MOUNTAIN MAN'S FIRST TIME

MEN OF MAPLE MOUNTAIN BOOK SIX

SADIE KING

LET'S BE BESTIES!

A few times a month I send out an email with new releases, special deals and sneak peeks of what I'm working on. If you want to get on the list I'd love to meet you!

You'll even get a free short and steamy romance when you join.

Sign up here:
www.authorsadieking.com/free

MOUNTAIN MAN'S FIRST TIME

It's only ever been her...

I've been in love with Ursula Riley ever since I was twelve years old. I've watched her grow from a grief-stricken child to a strong and beautiful woman.

When she went away to college, I thought my feelings would cool. But now she's back, with plenty of sass and curves that make my blood run hot.

The problem is her big brother Bear. He's my best friend and her guardian, and he's fiercely protective.

He'd kill me if he knew what I was up to with his little sister...

Mountain Man's First Time is a forbidden love, dual virgins romance featuring an OTT mountain man who falls for his best friend's curvy little sister. No cliffhangers and a happily ever after guaranteed.

www.authorsadieking.com

1

KIT

"She's here."

The whisper travels down the wooden pews of the church to where I'm standing at the altar next to Bear.

He exhales nervously as the distinctive chords of the wedding march fill the old weather-beaten church.

The bridal party starts down the aisle with Colette on the arm of her father. She's beaming, looking radiant on her wedding day, and Bear gives a happy sigh.

But it's not Colette that I'm looking at. Walking ahead of the bride in a simple blue dress that hugs her curvy figure is Ursula. The maid of honor—Bear's little sister and the woman I've been in love with since I was twelve years old.

Her hair is piled high on her head. There are tiny flowers woven through it, and a few wisps hang down, framing her face. She looks so stunning that for a moment I can't breathe.

"She's beautiful, isn't she?"

Bear's talking about Colette, but I only have eyes for the bridesmaid.

"Yes. Yes, she is."

The bridal party reaches the front, and Colette takes her place next to Bear. A look passes between them that's so full of love it makes my heart ache.

I'd do anything to have Ursula look at me like that.

I steal a sideways glance at Ursula, and she must feel my gaze on her because she looks across at me and catches my eye.

She gives me a small smile. Her eyes are glistening, and I can tell she's as happy for Bear as I am.

He's had a tough ticket since their parents died eight years ago. Bear took over the running of the family brewery and became responsible for his younger sister.

Which is why my feelings for her are so impossible. It's why I've kept myself in check all these years.

It was torture when Ursula went away to college, as I wondered if she'd come back with some smart college boy in tow.

But in the months that she's been back, still single and with her figure filled out in voluptuous curves, it's been getting harder and harder to hide my feelings.

I try to concentrate on what the pastor is saying, but my gaze keeps straying back to Ursula.

She's watching Bear and Colette, and my gaze lingers on her profile, admiring her rosy cheeks and bright eyes. Her lips are painted a pale pink, making them look plump and kissable. I've never seen her look so beautiful or seen so much of her cleavage. But that dress seems to float just above her luscious, pillowy…

Bear nudges me, and I pull my attention back to the ceremony. Everyone's looking at me, but I've got no idea what's just been said.

"The rings."

The pastor looks at me pointedly, and I grab the box out of my pocket. Bear shakes his head at me. "You had one job…" he mutters under his breath.

I hand over the rings, and the ceremony continues.

I steal a glance at Ursula. She's got her hand over her mouth, stifling a laugh. Her eyes dance, and I grin back. I know I'm not going to hear the end of it from Bear, but at least I made Ursula smile at me.

"I pronounce you man and wife," says the pastor. "You may kiss the bride."

There are cheers from the audience as Bear lifts Colette off her feet and practically devours her face in a passionate kiss.

Ursula puts her fingers in her mouth and whistles, and I cheer loudly with the rest of them.

When the happy couple breaks apart, they're both smiling widely, and I feel a pang in my heart.

I want this. I want this kind of happiness.

I've never told Ursula how I feel. She was too

vulnerable after her parents' deaths. Then she went away to college, and I thought the feelings would fade, but they didn't. I thought Bear would chill with his overprotectiveness, but he didn't. He's made it clear what he'll do to anyone who messes with his sister.

I once saw him lay a guy out at his bar because he touched her ass while they were dancing.

I've sat on the sidelines, and I've waited. But looking at Ursula today, I realize I can't wait any longer. I want this kind of happiness, and I want it with her.

It's time to let her know how I feel.

2

URSULA

The last spoonful of chocolate mousse slips into my mouth and I close my eyes, savoring the taste as it melts on my tongue.

When I open my eyes, Kit's staring at me from his place at the table two seats down.

His eyes are focused on my mouth, and I wipe my finger across my lips, wondering if I left chocolate smeared all over them. That's the only reason I can think of for why he'd be staring at me so intently. Kit—my big brother's best friend and the guy I've had a crush on ever since I can remember.

Too bad any interest he's ever taken in me is like that of a second big brother, as protective of me as Bear is.

I wiggle my spoon at Kit. "Did you try the mousse?"

He cocks his ear at me, straining to hear above the rock music that's blaring from the speakers. If this is the chilled-out dinner music, I hate to think what the band's going to play.

"Did you try the mousse?" I try again, but he shakes his head and pushes his chair back.

Bear and Colette's seats are between us, but they're doing the rounds of each table, saying hello to their guests before the dancing starts.

Kit sits in the chair next to me, and my body tenses. He looks so hot in his tuxedo with his beard neatly trimmed. As a ranger on Maple Mountain, it's not often I see him out of his casual mountain wear.

"The mousse"—I hold up my empty bowl— "was delicious."

He gives me a sideways look, and I feel my cheeks going pink. I've got the man I've crushed on all my life in front of me, yet I'm talking about mousse.

"I'm more of a crumble man myself."

I cock my head to the side. "I never knew that about you."

"Oh, yeah. Give me a homemade apple crumble, and I'm a happy man."

If only it was that simple. I have a vision of turning up at Kit's cabin with a crumble straight out of the oven. Maybe that's what I need to do to get his attention.

"How's it going at the tourist office?"

I screw my nose up. When I got back from college six months ago with a degree in North American history, I'm not sure what I was expecting to do in the small mountain town of Maple Falls. I must be the most overqualified tourism board rep in the county.

"It's fine, just a little…" I shrug, not sure how to explain what I've been feeling. I'm restless in Maple Falls. I worked my ass off for this degree, but most of my time is spent directing tourists to the local toilets.

"…boring."

"You think you'll stick around?"

He asks it casually, but the look he gives me is anything but casual. My breath catches in my throat. Does he really care what I do, or is it an older brother's concern?

"It depends." On you, I want to add.

Just then Bear comes up to the table, his hand firmly clasped in Colette's. They're so happy together; my big brother looks like he's on cloud nine.

"It's first dance time. You two ready?"

I glance at Kit, feeling shy. As best man and maid of honor, we're supposed to take to the floor after Bear and Colette.

"Sure." Kit clasps my hand as he stands up.

Bear looks at our hands and scowls. "It's a first dance, not a date."

Colette pulls him away before he has time to say anything else, and Kit keeps his hand firmly in mine.

I'm relieved he doesn't back down because of Bear.

"Still far too protective of you, I see."

To say my older brother is protective is an understatement. I've never even tried to bring a guy home to meet him. Not that there's been anyone I'd want to bring home, though. Only Kit.

"I'm hoping now that he's married, he might chill out a bit."

Kit's hand tightens in mine.

"Why? You got someone you want to date?"

Do I imagine the jealous look that flickers across his face? I decide it must just be his overprotectiveness again.

"Maybe," I say playfully, which earns me a scowl.

By now we're at the dance floor. The reception is at Bear's Brewery, and a makeshift dance floor has been put down, the place decorated in fairy lights. The rock music from earlier is replaced by Frank Sinatra.

"How did he get so graceful?" Kit whispers as Bear glides across the dance floor, expertly twirling Colette. "Has he been taking lessons?"

Bear will kill me if I let on he's been taking dancing lessons, so I just shrug, but Kit reads the twinkle in my eye.

He raises his eyebrows. "The things people do…"

It's true. Bear has mellowed out since he's been with Colette, and I like my brother mellow. But is he mellow enough not to freak out if I make a move on Kit tonight? Because I don't think I can hold back any longer.

The chorus finishes, which is our que to lead the other guests onto the floor.

Kit takes my right hand and slides his other hand

around my waist. As we step onto the floor, he pulls me toward him.

There's a rush of heat through my body, and I look into his eyes. They're staring right back at me, the pupils wide and intense.

I don't know how to ballroom dance, but with Kit leading the way, we sashay around the dance floor, letting Sinatra guide us.

"You look beautiful tonight, Ursula."

To hear my name on his lips makes my body tingle. Everyone just calls me Urs, but I like my full name. It means bear in Latin, and that makes me feel strong.

"Thank you."

If it were anyone else, I would think they were drunk, but I know Kit never has more than one or two beers.

"You clean up well too."

He grins. "I had my beard trimmed and shaped."

"I can tell." What I don't say is that I'd love to run my hands through his beard, feel it scratch against my skin. "I'm sure the ladies will take note."

I hope Kit doesn't notice the bitter note that comes into my voice. I've seen the way Colette's cousins have been looking at him tonight.

"There's only one woman I want to notice."

My breath hitches in my throat. The way he's staring at me dares me to hope that he's talking about me.

"Who's that?" I squeak.

"If you don't know that, then you're not as smart as I thought."

At that moment, he lets go of my waist and twirls me out to the middle of the dance floor, then reels me back in until my back is pressed against him and his mouth is next to my ear.

"You, Ursula. It's always been you."

His hot breath on my neck makes my hairs stand on end. At his words, my heart lifts, and there's a delicious tremor all the way down my spine and between my legs.

"Kit..." I breathe his name, but he spins me away again. This time when I come back to him, he grabs me by the waist, and I'm looking up into his eyes.

My body is pressed against his, and I feel something hard probing into my belly. Realizing what it is, there's a rush of liquid heat between my legs. My cheeks go red, and my panties dampen.

Kit opens his mouth to say something, but a thick hand suddenly clamps onto his shoulder.

"Getting a bit close there, buddy."

Bear wears a jovial smile, but I can see the tension behind his look. "Come to the bar with me. I want to celebrate my wife with tequila."

Kit gives me an apologetic look before he's whisked off to the bar.

Kit's words whirl around in my head, making my heart race and my body overheat. I need air, and I might need to change my underwear. Being so close to Kit has left pools of wetness between my legs.

My stuff's upstairs in Bear's apartment where I got ready for today with Colette. I head up for a quick breather, hoping to compose myself and change my sticky underwear.

3

KIT

"It's an awesome wedding, man."

We're followed to the bar by the camera crew. I never had Bear down as the sentimental type, but filming the wedding is the one thing he insisted on.

He waves the cameraman away. "Go video my wife, not me."

Bear's grinning as he slips behind the bar and grabs the top-shelf tequila. He snags two shot glasses and pours the liquid into them.

"A toast to my wife."

"To Colette."

We clink glasses, and I swallow the fiery liquid. It burns my throat, and I stifle a cough. I've never been good with shots, but it's my best buddy's wedding day so I've made an exception.

Bear slams his shot glass down on the table.

"When you are going to find yourself a wife, Kit?"

Bear is slightly blurry eyed from the alcohol, but he's in a good mood. Maybe this is the time to tell him about Ursula.

But what is there to tell? We were interrupted before I could find out how she feels.

"I've got my eye on someone."

He raises his eyebrows and looks around the wedding party.

"One of Colette's cousins? That redhead has been eyeing you all night."

I shake my head. "Nah, not my type." I've only got one type, only ever had one type, and her name's Ursula.

Bear narrows his eyes at me.

"Is it someone from town? Someone I know?"

"You could say that."

Aw, man. I'm not ready to have this conversation without being sure Ursula wants me too. Luckily, Colette comes looking for Bear before he can ask any more questions.

"Have you seen the guest book?"

Bear shrugs. "We have a guest book?"

She slaps him playfully on the shoulder. "It should be on the gift table, but I think I forgot to bring it down."

She starts to head off, and Bear grabs her by the wrist. "Stay and have a shot with me, wifey."

Colette giggles, and Bear grabs another shot glass.

"One was enough for me." I hold up my hand. "I'll go get the book for you."

Colette gives me a thankful look. "I think it's on the table upstairs."

There's a staircase behind the bar that leads straight up to Bear's apartment, and that's where I head now.

This is where the girls got ready today, and you can tell.

The air is filled with the smell of perfume and hairspray. Clothes trail across the floor. There are empty champagne glasses and strange looking hair styling tools lying on the table.

There's movement in the bedroom, and Ursula appears in the doorway.

"I didn't know you were up here." I don't want her to think that I followed her.

"I came to freshen up."

She sweeps a tendril of hair behind her ear; her finger grazes her throat, and I long to run my lips over the soft skin there. I swallow hard and force myself to look away.

"You see the guest book anywhere?"

"Try the table."

She moves to the table in the corner of the room, and I follow.

There's a leather-bound book that's being used as a shelf to display small pots of dark-colored powder that I think might be eyeshadow. My big hands feel clumsy among the delicate makeup pots as I move them out the way.

"Got it."

We've both been rummaging at the table, and when I hold up the book, I realize how close we are.

The tendril of hair has gotten lose again, and I slip it behind Ursula's ear.

She looks up at me with clear eyes that seem to see right into my heart.

"Urs…" My fingers run down her throat, feeling her pulse quicken under my touch. "Your skin's as soft as I imagined it would be."

Her hand comes up to stroke my cheek, her fingers running down to graze my beard.

"I've wanted to touch your beard for so long."

My heart melts at her touch, and her words make me bolder. I lay the book on the table, and my other hand slides around her waist. If Bear saw us now, he'd probably kill me. But I don't care.

We're inches apart. I can smell the sweet scent of her perfume mixed with freshly applied lip gloss.

My other hand slides up her cheek, cupping her chin in my hand. "And I've wanted to kiss you for a long time."

Her eyelids flutter shut and her lips part, inviting me in. My mouth presses against hers. She's warm and soft, and I breathe her in. All thoughts of Bear are forgotten. It's just the two of us now as my body shifts against her and my whole universe realigns with a kiss.

4

URSULA

armth radiates from my lips and spreads through my body as Kit's mouth slowly explores mine.

I've dreamt about this moment for so long. Ever since I was a little girl kissing my pillow and pretending it was Kit.

Now we're finally kissing—the moment I've longed for—and my body is heating up fast. Kit moves his mouth to trail down my throat, his warm breath tickling my neck and sending shock waves buzzing all the way between my legs.

A moan escapes my lips, and I grind my hips against him. There's a pull in my core that's been building for years and can't be ignored any longer.

His hands tangle in my hair, and he pulls my head back so our eyes meet.

"I've waited a long time for this, Ursula."

My hand slides down his front until I find the bulge in his pants. I tug gently and he groans, his eyes rolling closed and the sound sending shocks of heat to my pussy.

"Kit, I want you."

His eyes open. They're hooded and dark with desire. "Not like this Urs. The first time should be special."

He's right. There's something tasteless about making out at my brother's wedding. But now that I'm in his arms, I can't stop.

"Isn't this special?" I run my hand over his cock, stroking him through the fabric. He groans again, and I know I've found his weakness.

A struggle plays out on his face as his hand closes over mine.

"I won't take advantage of you when you've been drinking." He pulls my hand away from his trousers.

"I had a glass of champagne getting ready and another glass with the speeches, but you should know I'm not a big drinker. Anyway"—I slide my hand back to his trousers— "I want you to take advantage of me."

He closes his eyes as I stroke him.

"I want you to do all the things that you've been imagining to me."

"Oh God, Ursula," he practically growls. "You have no idea."

"I want this Kit; I want you."

I see the moment his resolve breaks, and it feels like victory.

His mouth meets mine, and this time, it's urgent. A passionate kiss. My pussy's on fire as his hands run down my back and ass, pulling me toward him.

With one arm, Kit clears a space on the table. Then he lifts me up by the waist and sets me down, hitching up the satin fabric of my bridesmaid dress.

"This isn't how I imagined the first time," he says as his fingers trail up my thighs.

Maybe he's right. Doing it at a wedding reception is a cliché, but I'm so overcome with need for him that I don't care. I wrap my legs around his waist and pull him toward me while my hands fumble with his belt.

"I have to tell you something," he says.

My breath catches in my chest, and I wonder what the hell he's going to say. But at that moment, the door bursts open, and Bear storms into the room.

5

KIT

We spring apart, but it's too late. Bear takes one look at us and the grin slides off his face.

"What the fuck?"

"It's not how it looks."

Ursula slides off the table, pulling her dress down.

I'm fumbling to redo my belt, but there's no disguising the hard-on that's sticking out.

"Did you fuck my sister?"

Ursula winces at the words, and I don't blame her. It's not how I would describe what we were about to do.

"That's not a nice way to say it."

There's a dangerous flash in Bear's eye, and before I can defend myself, he crosses the room, his fist connecting with my nose.

There's a stab of pain and a crack that probably means it's broken.

"Fuck, man…"

Blood pours out of my nose and onto my white shirt. But I don't fight back. I'll let Bear have that one.

"We didn't do anything. Not that it would be any of your business."

His eyes flash in anger.

"Of course it's my business. She's under my protection." He turns away in disbelief. "How long has this been going on?"

I'm pissed that it's any business of Bear's. But he was always going to be a problem. I just would have preferred to tell him rather than have him walk in on us.

"It was just tonight. Just one night."

Ursula crosses her arms and fixes me with a look that's as angry as her brother's.

"Just one night, was it?"

Shit. Now I've managed to piss off both Riley siblings.

"That's not what I meant."

Bear's look of fury is back. "How dare you mistreat my sister."

He comes at me again. This time, I'm angry. I'm pissed that he thinks I could mistreat Ursula, that he thinks that badly of me.

My aim is low as I swing my fist, landing a hit in his stomach. Bear doubles over, grabbing his waist.

"Kit!" Ursula exclaims, and I hear the shock in her voice.

Bear recovers and lunges at me. I duck, grabbing him around his substantial waist.

I'm a big buy, but I'm not as big as Bear. We wrestle, grasping each other, neither willing to give any ground.

"For God's sake, stop it!"

Ursula pushes between us, and we're forced to break apart.

"Stop behaving like children!" She stands between us with her hands up. "This is a wedding. Don't turn it into a brawl."

We eye each other warily.

"I was looking out for you," Bear says. She cuts him off.

"I don't need you to look out for me, Bear. I'm twenty-two years old. I can make my own decisions."

He's breathing hard, still seething.

"I told you you're too protective."

She turns her chastising gaze to me. "And I don't need you to defend me either. You're a mess, Kit. You've got blood all over you."

She turns back to Bear. "What do you think Colette would say if she knew about this?"

Bear drops his head.

"I will not have you ruin my new sister's wedding day. Pull yourself together."

"Kit." Her eyes snap back to me, and I look at her hopefully. "Go home and clean yourself up."

"But…"

She puts a hand up to silence me. "No, Kit. I don't want to hear it. I've had enough of the both of you."

Her eyes flash with anger, and I know there's no point trying to talk to her tonight. Besides, she's right, I can't go downstairs with blood all over myself.

"I'll call you," I say. But she shakes her head, still looking pissed off.

I don't blame her. I practically ravished her and then punched her brother in the guts. What a way to win a woman over.

I head out the back door of Bear's feeling like the biggest ass in the world.

The buzz of my phone pierces through my throbbing temples. Scrambling for it, I come awake quickly and press it to my ear.

"Ursula?"

"Is this Kit?" The male voice sounds uncertain.

"Yeah." I can't hide the scowl from my voice as I swing my legs over the side of my bed and hold my head in my hands.

The punch Bear landed didn't break my nose, but it sure gave me a headache. I rub my temples, trying to make sense of what the guy on the other end of the phone is telling me.

"Some hikers went up the mountain yesterday, and they haven't come back."

That sobers me up. "How many?"

The guy gives me the details, and I'm already getting dressed as I hang up the phone. As ranger on Maple Mountain, this is what I'm trained to do.

I swallow a couple of painkillers for my head then pull my boots on.

Before I go, I check the messages on my phone. There's nothing from Ursula, only the seven texts I sent her last night apologizing for my part in the scuffle with Bear.

If I'm heading up the mountain, there won't be any signal, and I don't know how long I'll be. She doesn't answer my call, so I leave a quick message and head off to find the lost hikers.

6

URSULA

The suitcase strains under my weight but sitting on it is the only way to get the zips anywhere near each other. After a struggle with the zipper, I finally tug the suitcase closed.

I've been living in the family cabin since I got back from college, and I give it one last look as I wonder when I'll be back.

I'm dragging my suitcase downstairs when there's a knock at the door.

Kit's standing on the porch looking tired and anxious. My heart breaks to see him like that, but I take a deep breath, remembering my resolve.

"Can I come in?"

He never used to have to ask to come into our place. But today he hesitates like he's not sure he's welcome.

I open the door wide, and he brushes past me. His

scent of pine needles and woodsmoke is so familiar it makes my heart ache.

He looks rough, like he hasn't slept, and there's a purple bruise above his nose.

"You look like shit."

He half grins at me, and the tension falls from the air.

"I've been up the mountain. Some tourists thought it would be fun to stray from the trail and got themselves lost."

"I heard." I don't tell him I listened to his voice message ten times while I tried to make up my mind about what to do.

It's two days after the wedding, and I've been following the search knowing that Kit was leading it—and knowing that I can't stay in Maple Falls.

"You're leaving." He eyes the suitcase wearily.

"There's nothing for me here." Kit winces. I hate hurting him like this.

"I'm suffocating here, Kit. Bear means well, but I'm tired of him being so overprotective. I'm sure Dad would never have been like that."

Kit perches on the side of the couch. "He's scared for you, Ursula. That's why he's so protective. He was made responsible for you, and he takes that very seriously."

"I don't know why you're defending him after what he did."

Kit rubs his nose and winces at the pain.

"Yeah, he wasn't too happy to find us kissing."

I snort out a laugh. "Kissing? Another minute and we would have been..." I can't finish the sentence. Just thinking about it makes my body hot. My gaze meets Kit's, and he stands up and closes the distance between us.

"Stay, Ursula. Stay with me."

His gaze dips to my lips, and I so want to kiss him right now. But I pull back.

"And always have Bear breathing down our necks? No thanks."

He takes my hands in his, and the warmth of his touch makes me tremble. I want to stay with him, but it's impossible.

"Bear overreacted. I won't let him get between us."

"And I won't cause a family feud. Bear's all the family I've got left."

"Not all." His finger slides over my wrist, drawing circles on my skin and leaving a burning sensation that I feel deep in my core.

"You've got me. You've always had me."

"Don't make me choose, Kit. Don't make me choose between you and my brother."

His gaze is so intense I have to look away. I hate that I'm in this position. I hate that it can't just be easy.

"What if you didn't have to choose? Bear was mad, but I'm sure he'll get over it once he knows my intentions."

"And what are your intentions?" My heart's

hammering in my chest. This has all happened so fast that it doesn't seem real.

"I'm serious about you, Ursula. This isn't some casual thing. I want to be with you. Forever."

My breath hitches in my throat. It's everything I ever dreamed he'd say.

"I want that too." But it seems so unlikely, living here in harmony with my overprotective brother.

"I don't want to sneak around, Kit."

He rubs his nose. "And I don't want to get punched again. I'll go see Bear and smooth it over."

I hate that I have to get my big brother's blessing, but at the same time, it's nice he cares about me so much.

"Don't get hurt."

Kit growls. "I can hold my own, you know."

He pulls me toward him, and I feel the pure manly strength of him.

"Tell your nose that."

Kit laughs. It's the best sound in the world. He presses his lips against mine, and this time, it's a gentle kiss. Less urgent. But it still makes my body shiver. I press myself against him, my pussy aching for relief.

"I'm going to get Bear's blessing before this goes any further. I respect my friend enough to do that." He backs away. "And I don't want another bruise."

I watch him go, feeling lighter but anxious.

They don't call my brother Bear for nothing. If he

feels his family is in danger, he'll protect them to the death.

I only hope he can see that Kit isn't a threat. He's the one person in this world who could make me truly happy.

7

KIT

It's with trepidation that I climb the steps to Bear's place. The sound of laughter reaches me from inside, and I hesitate.

Bear and Colette are leaving for their honeymoon tomorrow, and they're probably busy packing.

But what I need to say can't wait. I knock on the door.

Colette opens the door. "Kit," she exclaims, eyeing my bruised face, "I had no idea it was that bad."

She gives Bear a dirty look, which means he told her what happened but probably not the whole truth.

Bear comes to the door and eyes me warily.

"What do you want?"

He's got a growl to his voice, but I've been his friend for too long; he doesn't scare me.

"To give you a chance to apologize, numbnuts."

His eyes widen in surprise, but he doesn't laugh at the insult like he usually would.

"Me? Apologize? You're the one that took advantage of my sister."

Colette holds up her hands. "Cool it, you two."

She has an immediate effect on Bear, and he looks away, the aggression fading from his expression.

"Kit, come on in." She steps out of the way, and I enter the house with Bear's gaze following my every move.

"Don't know why you're inviting him in. He attacked my sister. Do I have to lock my wife up too?" Bear mumbles, but Colette laughs.

"Oh, honey, I told you. Anyone can see Kit and Urs are crazy about each other. Give the man a chance."

Bear folds his arms, but his look softens. "Is this true?" he asks.

"Yes," I say simply. "I love her."

Bear snorts and looks away. Colette claps her hands together. "Told ya," she says gleefully. "I need to pop out for some milk. I'll leave you two guys to talk."

She pulls her coat on while Bear and I eye each other.

"No fighting, okay?" She kisses Bear lightly on the forehead. Her breezy manner contrasts with the frown carved into his face.

Once the door shuts behind her, he doesn't hold back.

"How long has it been going on?" he demands.

"I've loved your sister ever since I can remember."

His eyes narrow. "So, you've been sneaking around without telling me?"

"Nah, man. Give me some credit. I only told her how I feel at the wedding." I think back to that kiss, her body pressed against mine. "Lucky for me, she feels the same."

Bear grunts. "Looked like you were taking advantage of her to me."

"You ever know anyone to take advantage of your sister? She's got no problem speaking her mind, and she's as tough as you are."

Bear huffs again, but I can tell I'm getting through to him.

"We love each other. This isn't casual. I want to be with her. I want to marry her."

That gets his attention. He squints at me as if looking at me for the first time, and I don't see my friend. I see the head of the household trying to do the right thing for his family.

"Why do you think you deserve her?"

"Come on, man. You know me. I've been there for the both of you through the hard times. I've got a steady job. I can provide for her." Fuck, this feels weird, selling myself to my best friend. But if that's what it takes to win Ursula, I'll do it.

"There's space in my cabin, and I've got designs approved for an extension. A couple of extra rooms for kids."

He holds his hand up. "Slow down, man. Don't talk to me about kids."

He seems to be softening, but his voice hardens with the next question.

"How about other women?"

"What other women?"

"I've seen the tourists that come through here, the women falling over you at the bar. You really gonna give all that up? God knows how many of them you take back to your cabin."

He's got this dead wrong. "None."

"You expect me to believe that?"

"Yeah, because that's the God-honest truth. I've never taken anyone back to my cabin." I take a deep breath. It's time he knew how serious I am.

"I've been saving myself for Ursula."

Bear stares at me. "Come again?"

"I've never been with anyone." His mouth drops open in disbelief.

"When I realized she was the woman I was gonna marry, I never wanted to be with anyone else."

He's shaking his head in disbelief. "You telling me you're a virgin?" I nod. "Urs know about this?"

"Not yet."

He looks away, a slight smile on his face. "That's some fucked up shit."

"You want to talk about fucked up? I see you and Colette with the cameras all the time."

Bear's face reddens, and I know I'm onto something.

"It's cool, man." I hold my hand up, wondering if I've gone too far. "I don't know what you do, and I don't want to know. Just saying. Everyone has their kink, right?"

He stares at me so intensely that I think he's going to hit me again. Then he erupts into a belly laugh that makes his whole body shake.

"You know about the cameras?"

"I know something about cameras, man. Like I said, don't want to know details. That's your private shit."

Bear slaps me on the back, and I laugh along with him. The tension in the air dissipates, and I know I've got my buddy back.

"So, do I have your blessing?"

His hand is still on my shoulder, and I wait for him to crush me. "I suppose if she has to be with someone, I'd rather it was you."

I let out a big breath I didn't know I was holding. It's the only blessing I'm ever going to get out of him, and I'll take it.

He squeezes my shoulder tight, his face turning hard. "But you hurt her, you break her heart, I swear to God I will come for you."

Then the grin's back on his face, and he's laughing again.

"I gotta go, man. I've got a question to ask your sister."

He fixes me with a serious look. "You tell anyone about the cameras, and I'll skin you alive."

"You tell anyone I'm a virgin, same goes."

We slap each other on the back, and Bear pulls me in for a man hug. "You treat her well, okay?" There's a wobble to his voice, and I know that deep down, under his growly demeanor, he's just a man who wants the best for his family.

8

URSULA

As soon as I hear Kit's car pull up, I throw open the door. He steps out of the car, and I'm relieved to see there's no blood. That's got to be a good sign.

"Well?" I'm impatient to know what happened.

Kit saunters onto the porch and slides an arm around my waist. Having him close makes my insides melt and heat travel through my body.

"We have your brother's blessing."

Kit smiles at me, but it's a weird thought.

"We have Bear's blessing to…have sex?"

Kit throws his head back and laughs. It's the best sound.

"We have his blessing to get married."

His words make me gasp. I may have dreamed of marrying Kit for as long as I can remember, but now that he's asking, I'm stunned into silence.

Kit drops to one knee and takes my hand in his, his fingers running over my knuckles.

"Ursula, I've only ever wanted to be with you. You're beautiful, smart, funny, and courageous. I've known since I was a boy that you'd be my wife. Will you marry me?"

There are tears in my eyes, and I blink quickly. Kit is looking up at me so sincerely, so full of love.

"Yes! Of course I will."

I jump into his arms, almost toppling him over, planting kisses all over his face.

"Whoa, slow down. Let me put this ring on you."

He slides the ring onto my finger, and I hold my hand out, admiring the simple single diamond design.

"It's beautiful."

"So are you."

His words melt my heart, and I lean into his chest, a light, happy feeling overtaking my body. Kit slides an arm under my knees, and I squeal as he lifts me up.

He pushes the front door open with his shoulder, causing it to bang against the wall.

"Where are you taking me?"

"Upstairs. We have unfinished business."

There's a hint of a smile on his lips, and I giggle, knowing exactly what he means.

We reach my bedroom, and he throws me gently on the bed. I roll onto my side, leaning on one elbow as I watch him pull off his boots.

Kit peels off his sweater, and he's wearing a tight t-shirt underneath. It stretches across his chest, showing off his muscular frame. I sit up and run my hands over his chest, my legs dropping on either side of him.

Kit kneels on the bed, and I hook my thumbs under his t-shirt and peel it off.

I've seen his body so many times over the years, but this is the first time I've had a reason to touch it.

My fingers rake over his chest, feeling every muscle in his torso. I brush his nipples with my fingertips, and he sucks in a sharp breath. Finding a sensitive spot, I tug on his right nipple, and he groans.

"That feels nice."

A giggle escapes my lips. "I didn't know men have sensitive nipples."

He grins. "Neither did I."

Kit pushes me gently on the bed, and I fall backwards as he climbs on top of me. "Let's see whose are more sensitive."

I like the sound of that. I like the feel of it more as his hand slides up my top. Pulling my bra down, he cups my breast, his thumb brushing my nipple. It's a bundle of nerves that shoots tiny shock waves through my body and makes me shudder all the way down to my core.

A moan escapes my lips, and I open my eyes to see Kit staring intensely at me.

"I like it when you make that noise."

My whole body is on fire as he peels off my top. His gaze roves hungrily over me, taking in my breasts and body. Kit must have seen me a hundred times in my swimsuit at the lake, but suddenly, I feel shy. My hand crosses over my stomach, and he pulls it away.

"You're beautiful, Ursula."

I love it when he says that, and I guess in his eyes, I am.

Kit climbs up next to me on the bed. "I have to tell you something."

My heart stops for a moment. This is where the fairytale ends. This is where he says it's all a joke, that he doesn't really mean it.

"Don't look so worried." He must read my expression because he takes my hand in his and kisses my palm.

"What is it, Kit?"

"I've never done this before."

He seems nervous, and I'm not sure what he's talking about.

"Never proposed to anyone?"

He chuckles. "That too. I mean I've never been with a woman before."

He looks down when he says it, like he's embarrassed.

"This is your first time?"

His gaze meets mine. "I was saving myself for you."

My heart melts. For all these years, the feelings I had for Kit, he had them too.

"So was I."

He kisses me then. Slow and deep. Our bodies move

together, pressing against each other. My hips grind into his. The friction as my pussy presses against his hardness makes my core ache.

Kit's hand slides up my leggings and runs over the damp heat between my legs. He peels my leggings and panties off, and I help him out of his remaining clothes.

We lie naked, our bodies moving together. My hands run over the smooth skin of his back, exploring every inch of him.

His touch makes me shiver as he explores my body, running his hands over every curve. Until, finally, his hands slide up my thighs and to my aching pussy.

His touch is gentle as his fingers graze my entrance, making me moan.

"You're so wet."

His voice is full of wonder, and I love that this is his first time too, that we're discovering this together.

My hand wraps around his shaft, and I move my palm back and forth, loving the way it makes him groan.

Kit moves on top of me, getting onto his knees. I part my thighs for him, and he slides his cock over my slit.

"We should use a condom," he says.

"Should we, though?" The thought of having Kit's babies is a massive turn-on for me, and when he meets my eye, I know he feels the same.

"Urs, are you sure?"

I nod. "I want to feel you. Kit. Every part of you."

He slides the tip of his cock into me, and already I feel so full. My hips arch, and he freezes.

"Am I hurting you?"

"No," I moan, "keep going."

But he keeps just the tip in as he leans forward, kissing my breasts and nipping my throat.

"I want to take it slow, Ursula. I need to take it slow, or I'll fucking explode just looking at your tight pussy."

The naughty words send a thrill down me. I've never seen this side of Kit before, and I love it.

"Say that again," I whisper.

His breath is hot on my neck as he whispers into my ear.

"I've waited a long time to fuck your tight cunt, Ursula."

As he says it, he slides into me, and I cry out. There's a sharp pain. Then I feel full as my pussy closes around his velvety cock.

"Kit." It's so intense I can barely breathe. "Fuck, it feels good."

"I know, baby." His voice is strained, and I realize he's barely holding it together. I want to make him lose control.

"You can come for me, Kit. Come inside my pussy."

"Fuuuuck."

He thrusts into me, and I grind my hips against him. His eyes squeeze shut, and he's about to lose control. It's the sexiest thing I've ever seen. Suddenly, the pressure that's been building inside me explodes.

"Kit! I think I'm coming."

"Come for me, baby."

My body shatters into a million pieces as I feel Kit explode inside me. He cries out my name as my pussy tugs at his cock, milking him dry.

It's the most amazing feeling in the world, and I dig my fingers into his back, pulling him close to me and clinging to him.

He holds me tight, pinning me down with his arms. We're joined together, our bodies shuddering as one. Finally, and forever, together.

Six years later…

"How's this for a surprised face?" I widen my eyes and drop my jaw, making Bear chuckle.

"Nah, man, too obvious. You gotta go like this." He puts his hands to his mouth and makes high pitched "oooooh" sound.

I laugh so hard that my eyes water. "I'm not making that noise. I want to get laid tonight."

The laughter drops off Bear's face instantly. "That's my sister you're talking about, bro."

I hold my hands up placatingly. "Calm down. Just messing around."

A grin breaks out over Bear's face. "Me too."

We both laugh, and he hands me the hip flask. I take

a swig of bourbon that burns all the way down my throat.

"You think they're ready for us?"

Bear checks his watch. "Urs messaged me ten minutes ago. They're ready."

I take my feet off the dashboard of his pickup truck. "What are we still doing here then?"

"Enjoying some peace and quiet."

Bear looks out at the mountain and raises the flask to his lips.

I know what he means. Family life can be hectic, and it's not often we get time with just the two of us anymore.

When Bear suggested an early morning fishing trip on the day of my birthday, I knew something was up.

It wasn't hard to get him to tell me about the surprise party that my wife has organized. And the fact that she practically fell over herself making sure I went, even though I didn't want to leave her with the kids on her own on my birthday.

"Come on. Let's go."

It's a short walk to Bear's Brewery which, from the outside, looks like it's closed for the day. If it wasn't for the toddler that's pulled the curtain back to peer out at us, I wouldn't know anything was up.

"That one of yours?"

Bear shakes his head. "Looks like an Amery to me."

He makes a show of unlocking the door and indicates for me to go inside first. As soon as I walk in, the lights flick on and everyone yells.

"Surprise!"

My eyes sweep the room until I find my wife. She's grinning at me, and I smile back, hoping I've pulled off the surprised face. "Did you do this?"

I stride up to her and slide my arms around her waist. She's got the baby pinned to her hip, and I give my daughter a kiss on the forehead. Then I give my wife a long kiss on the lips.

There are cheers from the crowd, and someone wolf whistles.

"Happy birthday, Daddy."

Our three-year-old son pushes between us and hands me a piece of paper with colorful squiggles all over it.

"I made a card."

"Thank you, buddy."

I scoop him up in my arms, and he squeals with delight.

"And thank you," I whisper into Ursula's ear.

"Happy birthday, man." Ewan slaps me on the back, and I turn to shake his hand. "Ye catch any fish for the barbecue?

"Aye," I say, imitating the Scotsman. "We've got fresh trout."

A child runs between us, chased by an older kid, and Ewan calls out a warning to them.

"Have a birthday drink." Chase hands me a beer, and I take it gratefully.

His older brother Rowan is here too, looking less sullen these days now that he's got a wife and children.

Even Colton and Annie have come down the mountain with their brood of wild kids.

Ursula slips her arm around my waist, and I look around the room, a feeling of contentment in my heart.

It's full of friendly faces. My mountain community. I wouldn't want to be anywhere else.

MEN OF MAPLE MOUNTAIN

Complete the Men of Maple Mountain series for your swoon worthy OTT alphas.

Each book is a standalone but best enjoyed in together.

Men of Maple Mountain

Mountain Man's Obsession – Colette & Bear

Mountain Man's Captive – Annie & Colton

Mountain Man's Virgin – Brooklyn & Chase

Mountain Man's Muse – Heather & Kane

Mountain Man's Redemption – Bethany & Ewan

Mountain Man's First Time – Ursula & Kit

Companion titles

Mountain Man's Healer - Jenny & Rowan

All the Scars we Cannot See - Emily & Sam

Boxset Collection

Men of Maple Mountain Books 1-7

Includes a bonus short story:

Mountain Man's Steamy Anniversary - (Bear & Colette)

HIS BOUNTIFUL GIFTS

I conjured him out of the ocean, and now he claims me as his…

He washed up on the beach, cut and lashed by the storm, his body naked and marked with ink that tells of a dark past.

Ronan was my gift from the gods, my salvation. The one to save me from my fate.

He needs a place to hide, and my caravan becomes his safe haven—and I his willing nurse.

Until his past tracks him down, and the ocean calls back her gift…

His Bountiful Gifts is a forced proximity instalove romance featuring an OTT obsessed man and the curvy woman he claims as his own.

Keep reading for an exclusive excerpt or visit:
mybook.to/MSHisBountifulGifts

HIS BOUNTIFUL GIFTS

CHAPTER ONE

Ula

The pre-dawn sky holds no trace of the oppressive clouds from yesterday as I step out of my car and head down the walkway to the beach. The sea simmers and swirls, bubbling around rock pools and tugging at the shore.

The day after a storm is always my favorite time to walk along the beach and watch the foamy waves tug at the debris tossed onto the shore, as if they have no memory of the raging sea and devastation from the night before.

I woke before dawn and drove the two miles to the beach, eager to see what gifts the storm has brought me.

Sails are broken at the marina, and roof panels have

been blown off the small cluster of buildings along the Temptation Bay beachfront.

A cool breeze hits my neck, and I pull Gram's shawl tight around my shoulders. My bare feet sink into the ground, wet sand squelching between my toes as I start along the beach.

Driftwood, twisted and worn by the water, lies scattered across the sand as I pick my way along the shoreline.

There's a shape up ahead, perhaps a particularly large piece of driftwood that the tide has thrown up onto the shore.

In the brightening dawn light, it appears more like an animal, maybe a seal that's swam too far south. Or a small whale separated from its pod and beached in the storm.

As I approach the object, the sun breaks the horizon, casting her first golden rays across the sand.

My breath hitches in my throat. It's not a seal. It's not a whale, and it's certainly not a piece of driftwood.

The storm has brought me a man.

Pale light creeps over the figure lying on his back on the sand. I take a few steps closer, peering curiously at him.

His shoulders are massive, the size of small boulders. Seaweed twists over taut muscles and dark ink patterns that snake down his arms, around his wide chest, and down to his…

Oh my. I take a step back.

He's naked.

My throat goes dry, and I swallow hard.

There's a naked man washed up on the beach. I should run back to my car and call for help. But my curiosity is too strong.

Stepping forward, I allow my gaze to sweep his torso, taking in the ink that swirls and twirls in patterns of hidden meaning under a layer of chest hair.

My gaze follows the thin line of hair from his chest over his hard belly. Even while lying still, the outline of his abs can be seen. My eyes continue down to the mound of thick, curly hair and what lies beyond.

His member hangs thick and dark, curled down the side of one thigh like a sleeping sea snake.

A gasp escapes my lips.

Because, yeah, it hangs halfway down his thighs now. What would this ocean giant look like hard? An image of his thick purple cock—hard as rock and dripping juice—jumps into my head.

There's a stirring in my core and a tug so strong I stagger to my knees. Dampness floods my panties, and I have to catch my breath.

The ocean has certainly been bountiful with her gifts this morning.

I tear my gaze away from the man's bounty to study his face. Dark hair is plastered to his cheeks, and his eyes are closed. His lips are tinged blue.

Shit.

Here I am fantasizing about his giant squid when the man might not even be alive.

Fear and a sense of loss flood me, which is stupid because I only found him a minute ago.

Reaching out to take his pulse, my fingers are about to press down on his throat when the man moves.

His hand shoots out of the sand and grasps my wrist, a movement so quick it makes me gasp.

My eyes flick to his face, and he's staring right at me, his eyes as blue and stormy as the ocean. The intensity of his look makes my pulse quicken and my core turn to liquid.

It feels like hours that his gaze is locked with mine, but it must only be a few seconds. Then his eyes move down my face to my mouth open with shock.

His look travels down my throat to my chest. I'm leaning over him, my top fallen open, and he must be able to see down my top to my breasts pushed together in the bra I shoved on this morning.

He takes his time looking me over, and I feel myself melt under his gaze.

I catch movement out of the corner of my eye, and I glance down his body. Between his legs, the giant sea snake is stirring to life. I'm transfixed, terrified and turned on all at once.

His cock unfurls and hardens, the length stretching out down his thigh. It's purple and thick and stirs feelings inside me I've never felt before. A need. A longing that none of the neighborhood boys have ever stirred in me.

I'm dripping wet, my breath coming in short, sharp pants. I let out a whimper.

The man groans, and my gaze darts back to his face. His eyes are dark and hooded. He croaks one word. "Mine."

Then his eyes close, his grip on my wrist loosens, and he falls unconscious onto the sand.

To keep reading visit:
mybook.to/MSHisBountifulGifts

GET YOUR FREE BOOK

Sign up to the Sadie King mailing list for a FREE book!

You'll be the first to hear about exclusive offers, bonus content and all the news from Sadie King.

To claim your free book visit:
www.authorsadieking.com/free

BOOKS BY SADIE KING

Maple Springs

Men of Maple Mountain

All the Single Dads

Candy's Café

Small Town Sisters

Fudge & the Firefighter

All the Scars We Cannot See

The SEAL's Obsession

What the Fudge

Sunset Coast

Men of the Sea

Sunset Security

Underground Crows MC

The Thief's Lover

Kings County

Kings of Fire

King's Cops

For a full list of titles check out the Sadie King website

www.authorsadieking.com

ABOUT THE AUTHOR

Sadie King is a USA Today Best Selling Author of short instalove romance.

She lives in New Zealand with her ex-military husband and raucous young son.

When she's not writing she loves catching waves with her son, running along the beach, and good wine, preferably drunk with a book in hand.

Keep in touch when you sign up for her newsletter. You'll even snag yourself a free short romance!

www.authorsadieking.com/free

FOLLOW ME ON BOOKBUB

Follow Sadie King on BookBub to get an alert whenever she has a new release, preorder, or discount!

www.bookbub.com/authors/sadie-king

* 9 7 9 8 2 1 5 7 7 3 3 6 9 *